The Wee Seal

Janis Mackay & Gabby Grant

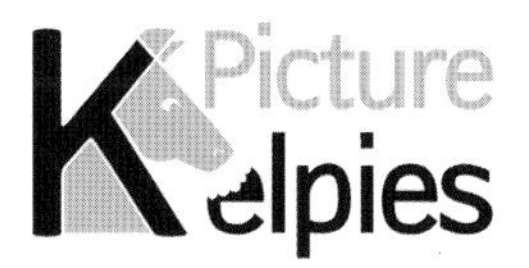

There's a strange white stone on the beach today.
It wasn't there before.
It came in the night
when the world was asleep,
that strange white stone on the beach.

The strange white stone hears a screeching gull
and the curlews loud by the shore.

Perhaps it isn't a stone at all?

In the still of night the white stone shifts,
and sniffs the salty air.

It has eyes, a mouth, a quivering nose…
It's a beautiful baby seal!

Honk! Honk! comes a call through the moonlit night. A dark seal slips from the sea. She rocks over sand, seaweed and shells to comfort her little one.

The pup suckles and snuggles in close.

Side by side they lie, all night.

At sunrise the mother returns to the sea.
She has fish to hunt, fat salmon and trout.
Be safe, wee seal. *Honk! Honk!*

The wee seal is alone on the sand.

But someone is watching.
Every morning Jamie, who lives
in the house by the beach, calls,
"Wake up, wee seal!"
And every night at bedtime,
"Sleep tight, wee seal!
Your mum will come."

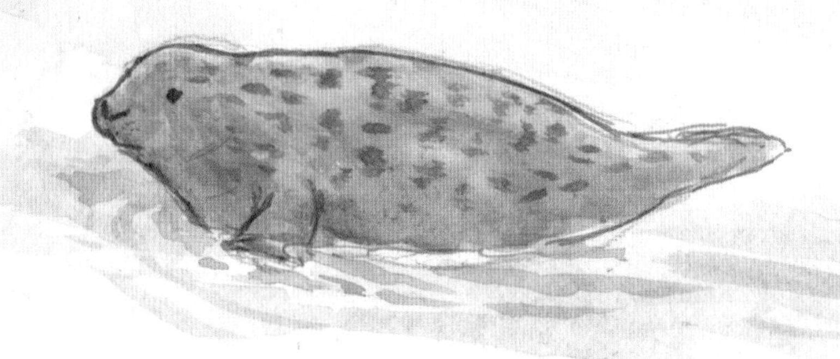

A busload of tourists
arrives at the beach.

"A seal!" someone squeals. "How cute! How sweet!" They take photos, point. "Poor thing's lost his mum," someone shouts.

They don't know she comes in the night
and stays with her pup till the morning light.

The wee seal whimpers.
The people jostle and bustle.
They're too loud and too close.

"Have a biscuit," says a girl,
thrusting out her hand. Then,

"Ouch!" she yells,

"The wild thing
bit my thumb!"

Jamie comes running with his arms stretched wide.

"Leave him alone!" he cries.

"The wee seal's ok.
His mum comes
in the night.
I made a sign."

The tourists
go away.

The sea washes in, the sea washes out.

There's a smooth black stone
on the beach one day.
The white seal pup has gone.

Jamie dashes outside.
The black stone looks up with sparkling eyes.

Scattered around, like snowflakes, lies the soft, white baby fur.
The wee seal is growing up.

Next morning a strange song wakes Jamie.

Woooooo-oooooooooo-hooooooooo

It’s a loud song, a deep song. The mother seal is calling from the sea. *Come in, wee one. It’s time.*

The wee seal slithers over seaweed. He bounces slowly over stones. He rocks all the way round a broken creel.

He's a brave seal, a bold seal, and his mother keeps calling.
Come in, wee one. It's time.

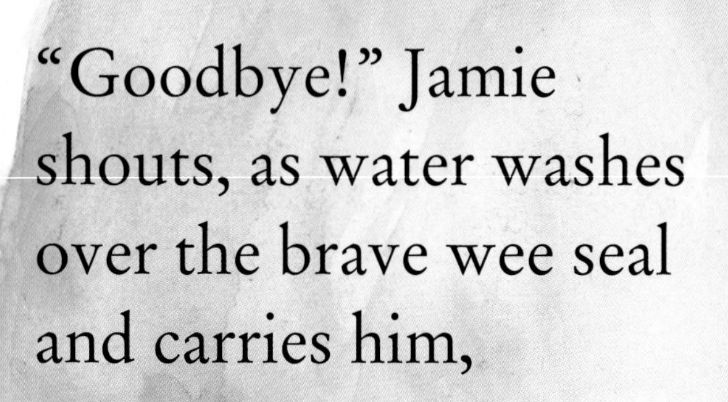

"Goodbye!" Jamie shouts, as water washes over the brave wee seal and carries him,

whoooosh!

out to sea.

Strong and free, he swims to his mother, who nuzzles her wee one's nose.

Side by side they glide.

There are two dark seals in the sea today.

Two dark seals gliding,
swimming together, in the
deep, blue, wonderful sea.

Honk! Honk! they cry. They flick back their tail fins. Are they waving to the shore?

Honk! Honk! Bye-bye!